This book belongs to:

....

....

For Dad, from Roo – R.S.
For Gemma and her Oz accent x – L.W

Published by Bonney Press,
An imprint of Hinkler Books Pty Ltd
45–55 Fairchild Street
Heatherton Victoria 3202 Australia
www.hinkler.com

BONNEY
PRESS

Copyright © 2015 QED Publishing
First published in the UK in 2015 by QED Publishing
A Quarto Group company, The Old Brewery, 6 Blundell Street, London, N7 9BH
www.qed-publishing.co.uk

Editor: Tasha Percy
Designer: Krina Patel
Editorial Director: Victoria Garrard
Art Director: Laura Roberts-Jensen

ISBN: 978 1 4889 3693 7
Printed and bound in China

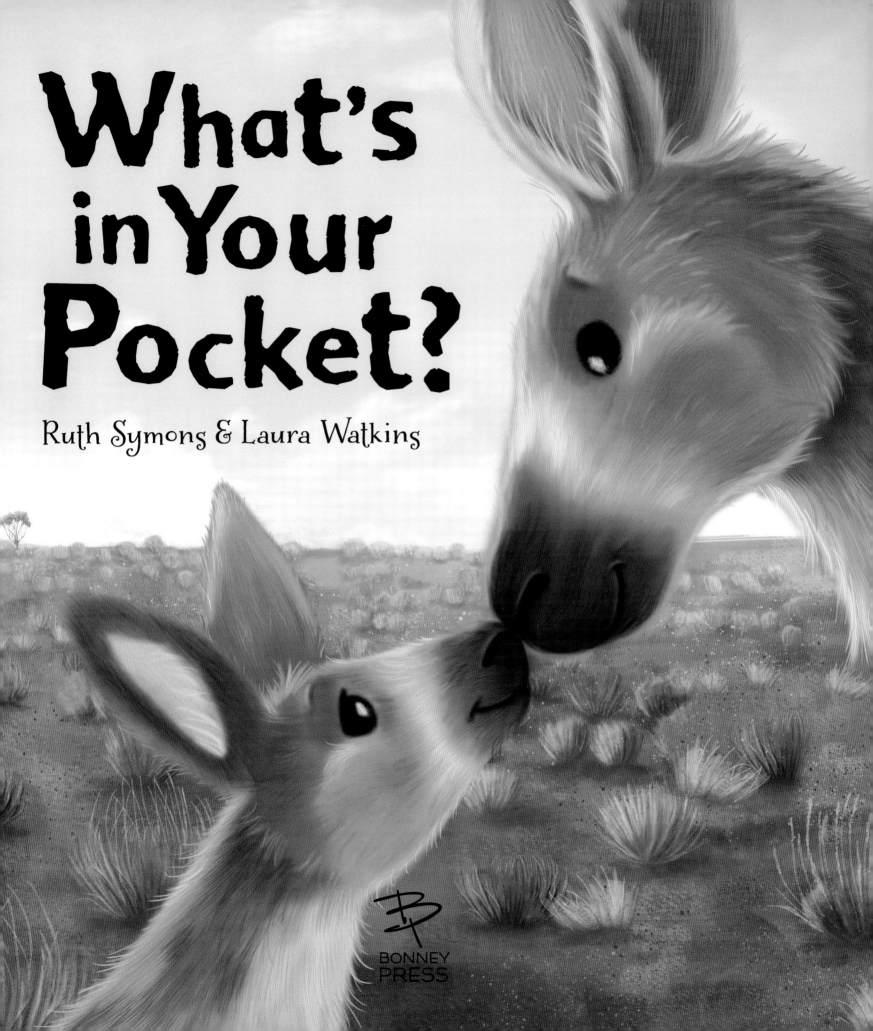

What's in Your Pocket?

Ruth Symons & Laura Watkins

BONNEY PRESS

Every day Josh **bounced** around with the other little joeys.

Every night he **snuggled** into
his mum's pouch.

It was a soft, warm pocket of fur –
the perfect place to sleep.

When Josh grew bigger Mum told him to
sleep on the grass. But Josh didn't want to.
He tried to climb into her pocket.

'No, Josh,' Mum said.
'There's no room.'

'Why not?
What's in your pocket?'
Josh asked.

'A surprise – something very special!
Try and guess what it is,'
she said with a smile.

'It's tiny, but it will grow bigger. You can play with it,
but not yet. It needs lots of love and care.'

'Will I like it?'
Josh asked the
next morning.

'Of course,' Mum said. 'You'll love it the minute you see it. It's the most **precious** thing in the world.'

Josh couldn't think what it could be,
so he went to ask his friends for help.

First, Josh **bounced** up to Katie the koala.

'Hello, Katie,' he said.
'Can you help me guess what's in Mum's pocket?
It's **tiny** but will grow bigger. And it's the
most **precious** thing in the world.'

Katie scratched
her shaggy ear,

'This eucalyptus tree started
as a **tiny** seed and grew bigger.
Its branches are my home and
its leaves are my dinner!'

'But the most **precious** thing in the world is right here on my back.'

Clinging to her back was a cute little koala baby.

'WOW', Josh said. 'That **is** precious.'

Next, Josh **bounced** up to Peter the parrot.

'Can you help me guess
what's in Mum's pocket?'
Josh asked.

'It's something I can **play** with,
but not yet. And it's the most
precious thing in the world.'

'Well I like to **play** with my friends, and sometimes I **play** the drums on this tree trunk.'

'But the most **precious** thing in the world is up there. Look!' Peter said.

Josh looked up at the top of the tree. A tiny parrot face was peering down from its nest.

'WOW', Josh said 'That **is** precious.'

Next, Josh tried Terry the termite. He was marching around his tidy termite mound.

'Hello, Terry,' said Josh. 'Can you help me guess what's in Mum's pocket?

It needs lots of **love** and **care**. And it's
the most **precious** thing in the world.'

'My termite mound needs lots
of **love** and **care**,' said Terry.

'It's my home, and
I've worked hard to make
it strong and safe.'

'But the most precious things in the world are the termites inside.'

Terry's friends and family all came out to wave at Josh.

'WOW', said Josh. They are precious!

Josh **bounced** back to Mum.

Whatever was in her pocket, it couldn't be a baby

koala, or a tiny parrot or a whole family of termites!

'I give up,' said Josh.
'What have you got in your pocket?'

'It's your baby brother,' said Mum.

A teeny tiny joey poked his head out. He was
small and delicate, and **very precious**.
Josh loved him the minute he saw him.

'WOW!' said Josh. 'That
is a good surprise!'

NEXT STEPS

Show the children the cover again. Could the children have guessed what the story would be about from just looking at the cover?

Josh can't guess what his mum has in her pocket. What did the children think it would be? Were they surprised at the end of the story?

Ask the children if they have ever been given a surprise. What is the best surprise that they can think of? What do they think is the most precious thing in the world?

Play a simple guessing game in pairs. One child thinks of an animal and gives the other child three clues to guess what it is.

Do any of the children have a baby brother or sister? Do they treat them with lots of love and care?

Do the children recognise any of the animals in the story? Do they know what country they all live in? Can the children think of any other animals that live in Australia?

Talk about kangaroos. A baby kangaroo is called a 'joey'. It lives inside its mum's pouch to keep it warm and safe. It will live there until it is about eight months old.

Ask the children to act out their favourite animal in the story. Can they jump like Josh, play the drums like Peter or march around like Terry?